ADVENTURE DUCK

VS

POWER PUG

BY STEVE COLE

ILLUSTRATED BY ALEKSEI BITSKOFF

ORCHARD

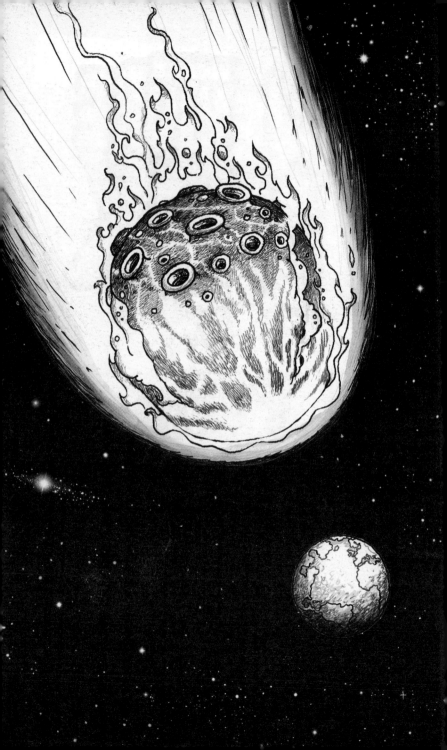

PROLOGUE
Pleased to Meteor!

From outer space, it came: a rock.

A glowing rock.

A glowing rock as big as an apartment block!

For billions of years, this giant glowing rock – this *meteor* – had been tumbling through the cosmos, brimful of mysterious powers. Now, for the first time ever, something was blocking its way ...

A small blue planet, called Earth.

- - - - - - -

The meteor couldn't miss. It glowed brighter and brighter as it plunged through the skies. Finally –

BOOM!!

– it burned up and broke apart into hundreds of fireballs, and they showered down all over the world. One fragment struck a barn in the middle of a farm.

CRASH!

Another streaked down into a watering hole in Africa.

SPLASH!

Yet others landed in Arctic snowdrifts, and deep in the rainforests of South America.

FWOMP! KA-BOOM!

But the biggest lump of glowing rock plunged down towards a small duck pond in a large park. Terrified ducks heard its warning whistle from the clouds and flew away, just in time. The meteorite struck the water with a steaming, sizzling

SPLOOSH!

The duck pond bubbled and boiled, and the ground shook. A nearby nest was thrown through the air and landed with a thump at the water's edge. **AMAZINGLY, THE EGG INSIDE DIDN'T BREAK**. It lay there among the twigs, pale and perfect.

The pond pulsed with light as energy ebbed from the mysterious meteorite.

And slowly, the egg began to glow too ...

A Boiled Egg

There was one duck at the park who didn't even notice when the meteorite struck. He was too busy hunting through a litter bin for sandwich leftovers. The ground beneath him rumbled with the **mega-rock's** shockwaves, but he put it down to indigestion.

"Whoa, pardon me!" he quacked, rubbing his full belly. "I'd better lie down for a bit."

Most ducks in the world think of themselves as 'A Duck'. This is because very small children, when taken to visit ponds, will often point and say, "Look – it's *A Duck*!" Some ducks decide the 'A' stands for 'Adam' or 'Alisha' or 'Amari', but this particular duck decided that his 'A' stood for *Adventure*. He was a bit of a show-off, as ducks go, and liked to stand out. Sometimes, he would call himself A.D. just so people would ask what the letters stood for.

"My name is Duck," he would say. **"ADVENTURE DUCK!"**

- - - - - -

Mostly, his adventures consisted of flapping or waddling about the park in search of tasty snacks left behind by park-goers.

At least, they did until today ...

A.D. arrived back at the pond to find it deserted. The water was gently bubbling like simmering soup. Something at the bottom shone spookily.

"COOL. A LIGHT SHOW!" cried A.D. He was so distracted, he tripped over something spiky and fell flat on his feathered face.

"It's a nest. And there's an egg in it!"

- - - - -

A.D. looked all about. "Hey, shouldn't someone be parking their butt on this thing?"

But there was no one around to answer.

The egg was pale green. When Adventure Duck touched it, his whole wing felt weirdly warm. "**WHOA!** It's a *boiled* egg," he said. Then he beamed. "It'll keep my tail feathers toasty while I take forty winks!"

Fluffing himself up, A.D. soon fell asleep on top of the warm egg. He fell asleep *so* quickly,

he didn't notice that the egg had started
to glow ...

When Adventure Duck woke up the next
morning, he felt different.

Good different.

He felt feathery-fit and full of energy.

As he got up, he almost trod on the egg
he'd been sleeping on. "Whoops!"

There the egg lay: pale green, with
speckles that sparkled.

"You're a funny-looking thing," said A.D.
"Where's your family, eh?"

Before he could study the egg more
closely, he noticed movement on the other
side of the pond. He noticed that the light
show in the water had gone out ... and
then he noticed a human child and her
father approaching with a plastic bag of
stale bread crusts.

"Look, Dad," said the child, pointing.
"A duck!"

ADVENTURE DUCK, the duck
thought hungrily, *and that bread will
be* **MINE!**

15

He flapped his wings to push himself across the pond – but went whooshing straight past the people and crashed head-first into an oak tree at incredible speed –

The tree fell down.

"Did you see?" gasped the girl to her dumbfounded dad. "That duck just knocked over a tree!"

How did I do that? A.D. scratched his head, which hardly hurt at all. *Oh, well,* he thought, *I'm sure some bread will help me figure it out.* He waddled towards the girl. Still in shock, she tossed him a piece of bread. A.D. jumped greedily to catch it ...

... and accidentally took off like a feathery firework, zipping into the sky!

WHAAAAAAAAA ... ?

Normally, A.D. couldn't fly higher than a few metres off the ground. Now he was up so high he almost bounced off a passing plane!

WHOA! he boggled, swerving to change course to avoid the jet. *I'm flying faster than a plane! What's happening to me?* A.D. was so shocked, he stopped flapping his wings – and started falling back down to earth! "**EEEK!**" He beat his wings again, zipping around in circles until eventually he hit the ground beside the duck pond and came rolling to a stop. He gave a quack of relief.

Only it came out as:

Without meaning to, Adventure Duck had let out a supersonic, super-enormous quack! Nearby houses shook and their windows rattled. Pigeons did somersaults. Fish were thrown from the pond and had to flip and flap about to plop themselves back in the water again. And the girl and her dad ran away with their hands over their ears as the sound echoed around the park at brain-blasting volume.

I must be quacking up! thought A.D. *I can't really be doing all these amazing things ...*

"But you ARE!" boomed a voice in reply.

- - - - -

Adventure Duck looked about sharply. "Who said that?"

"I DID!" the voice boomed – as the mysterious egg began to rise into the air!

A Hero Isn't Born!

Adventure Duck couldn't believe his eyes as the egg floated in front of him ... and suddenly grew a massive white moustache!

"Thank you for looking after me," said the egg in a calm voice. First one eye, then another, popped open

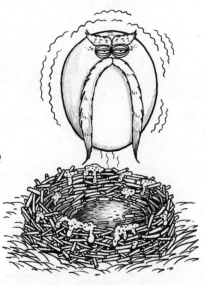

above the mega-moustache. "Without you, I might never have awoken."

"I think I must still be sleeping," said A.D. "This is just a **CRAZY DREAM**, right? It can't be real!"

"Perhaps reality IS a dream?" said the egg, waggling the bushy eyebrows that had suddenly appeared above its eyes. "Or perhaps a dream is now reality? Who can say?"

A.D. was flummoxed. "Er ..."

"*I* CAN SAY!" the egg boomed. "Before the meteorite struck this pond, I was

- - - - -

just another duck egg. But now I have absorbed its powers, I am **YOKI**! Yoki the wise! Yoki the wondrous! Yoki the all-round good egg."

"All-round **NUT**, if you ask me," said A.D. "What meteorite?"

"I will show you. I will place images in your mind!" Yoki's moustache began to quiver. "Just close your eyes ..."

Adventure Duck shut both eyes and gulped. He saw the meteorite landing in the pond. He saw the other ducks scattering, the pond-water boiling and bubbling, the abandoned egg glowing

- - - - -

in the nest ... then he saw himself last night, sleeping on it.

"Wow," he breathed.

"Ah," said Yoki. "Now you are beginning to understand."

"I understand ... that I am one good-looking fella! **WOO-HOO, YEAH!**" A.D. frowned. "Wait a minute – it looks as if **I WAS GLOWING TOO!**"

"You were." Yoki's voice zinged inside his ears. "As you sat upon me, we both absorbed some of the meteorite's mysterious energy."

- - - - -

"And that's why I can fly mega-fast, knock down trees and quack in supersonic style?"

"The meteorite affected us in different ways. You received great physical strength, while my mind was expanded," Yoki agreed. "And because you and I shared its energy, we are connected, now, through the power of **ESP!**"

Adventure Duck spluttered. "What?"

"*Egg-stra Sensory Perception*. That is how I can speak to you with just my mind," Yoki explained. "If you try hard, you can too."

"Forget it!" A.D. turned his back on Yoki.

- - - - - -

"Your brain must be scrambled, egg. I don't want to be connected to anyone. Bye!"

"No, you cannot go. My mystical senses tell me that the whole world is in danger!" Yoki rose higher into the air, as if riding an invisible cloud. "Another fragment of this meteor has created a mighty menace ... a fearsome four-legged foe. *We must work together to protect the Earth*."

"I don't want to work!" A.D. turned two triple somersaults in a single jump. **"I WANT TO PLAY!"**

"Hear me, duck. We now possess incredible powers ..."

- - - - -

"*I* possess incredible powers, you mean," the cheeky duck retorted. "*You* possess the need for a moustache comb and an extreme eyebrow-shaping kit." A.D. saw some more ducks waddling down the path on the other side of the park. "I think it's time to test these amazing abilities of mine some more!"

Before Yoki could say another word – **WHOOSH!** A.D. zoomed up to the startled ducks. "Hey, guys, how's it going? If you heard a very loud quack earlier, it was me, Adventure Duck ..." He opened his beak and let rip with a

QUACK!

(This second ear-crunching quack blew two park gates off their hinges. The other ducks jumped in the air, and then quacked in awe.)

"That's nothing!" Adventure Duck said, preening his feathers. "I knocked over a tree earlier. Pardon me while I stand it up again!" He raced over to the fallen tree and pushed it back upright again, grinding the trunk into the ground like an enormous fence post. "**TA-DAAAA!**"

THONK!

His excited audience made a commotion
of quacking and flapped their wings
in applause. Even a swan who was
notoriously hard to impress showed
an interest.

"After that, I expect you'd all like my
autograph. How about I just sign my
name in the sky so you can all see what
it looks like?"

With that, Adventure Duck took off
and flew nimbly enough to carve
his name clear across a cloud!

"Great goose-eggs above," groaned Yoki. "Of all the ducks who could have got amazing powers ... **THIS** is the one who has to save the world?"

Ducking Out

Adventure Duck couldn't wait to show off his new powers – to any animal he could find! He spent the next week flying all over the place in search of audiences to impress.

He landed beside a tractor in a field full of sheep.

"Hey, ewes!" said A.D. "Is this rust-heap blocking your view of me being awesome?" He lifted up the tractor, took off and dropped it again on the other side of the field. "**TA-DAAAA!**"

But the farmer who'd been sitting inside the tractor was furious and the sheep looked slightly baffled by the whole business, so A.D. took off and tried elsewhere.

He went to a wood and approached an animal with antlers. "Excuse me, my *deer*," he said. "Have you ever seen flying like this?" A.D. zoomed in and out of the branches of an enormous tree without snagging a single feather. He landed on the deer's back. "*Doe* you believe how cool I am?"

"Your feet are actually quite warm," the deer remarked.

A.D. flew off to a zoo and bent back the bars of the lions' enclosure with his wings. Then he flapped on to a lion's back and tried to ride it like a cowboy on a horse. "*Yeeee-hawwwww!*"

The lion sighed, refusing to budge. "If I

- - - - -

had superpowers like you, duck," he growled, "I would do *good deeds* instead of just showing off!"

"Then you'd be missing out. Showing off is FUN!" cried Adventure Duck, looping the loop as he flew away.

But over the next few days, showing off became less and less fun. People still pointed at him, shooting through the skies, and animals still applauded his antics. But truth be told, A.D. was starting to get bored. And he couldn't get the lion's words out of his head.

- - - - -

Perhaps he *should* use his powers to do good deeds?

Feeling a little bit homesick, he headed back to the park.

"So! You're back." Yoki floated up from behind a nearby bush, a stern expression on his shell. "Well, I hope you've got that silly showing off out of your system. You have startling powers, and with startling powers come—"

"Large amounts of soggy bread?" A.D. asked hopefully, his stomach rumbling.

"No! Well, yes. Sometimes." Yoki sighed.

"The point is that the lion in the zoo was right. You need to use your powers for good."

"Hey, wait. You were spying on me?" Adventure Duck scowled. "You nosy egg!"

"That is impossible," said Yoki. "I have no nose."

"How do you smell?"

"Like an egg." Yoki bobbed closer. "I told you, duck, thanks to the meteor our minds are connected. I can see through your eyes, hear through your ears, smell through your nose ..."

- - - - -

A.D. frowned. "Just tell me you don't wee through my—"

"**ENOUGH!**" boomed Yoki. "You must stop this tomfoolery. The danger that I sensed before has grown greater with each passing day – our foe-on-four-legs must be planning something terrible. If you are to stop disaster, you must become ... a hero. A *super*hero."

"A superhero, eh?" A.D. thought about this. "You know, you might be right. Being a superhero will REALLY impress the other ducks!"

Yoki sighed. "Well, I suppose that's a start."

- - - - -

He floated over to a patch of bulrushes.

"Come. There are things I must show you.

I have not been idle while you were away.

I have built a hidden base for us."

"Like a secret camp, you mean?

AWESOME!" A.D. jumped up and down.

"Where is it?"

"It lies beneath you!" Yoki smiled and

his moustache curled around one

of the bulrushes – it was, in fact, a

disguised lever. "Prepare to witness ... the

Underpond!"

He pulled on the bulrush – and the

ground flipped over!

- - - - -

"QUACK!" A.D. tumbled through empty space and landed in a pile of reeds and feathers. He was now in a muddy cave, damp and cool and lit with luminous pondweed. A small satellite dish pointed

up at the roof, connected with wires to a rusty old radio that squawked with static.

"Wow." A.D. gave Yoki a look. "Underpond? Under*pants*, more like!"

"We have all we need here," said Yoki defensively. "When my moustache senses danger I can tune this radio to hear what's going on anywhere in the world!"

"Whoopee!" said A.D. "It's all right for you – you're an egg-head. You can think deep thoughts anywhere." He started waddling up and down. "But me? I'll go crazy cooped up in this place. If I'm going to be a cool superhero then I need a cool pad."

Yoki looked confused. "A ... lily pad?"

"No, I mean 'pad' as in a place to hang out. With cool gadgets! And a big TV and a snack machine and stuff!" He paused.

- - - - -

"And a costume. I totally need a superhero costume!"

"There at least we agree." Yoki twisted a long reed sticking out of the floor. A hidden door in the wall swung open and whapped A.D. on the back of his head. "**Behold the built-in wardrobe!**"

Rubbing his sore head, A.D. looked inside and found a costume on a wooden hanger. There was a bright red cape, matching underwear and a white top with an 'A.D.' logo. "OK, that's actually pretty cool. Thanks, Egg. How long did it take you to make this?"

- - - - -

"Time ... is an illusion," Yoki said impressively, his moustache performing a small Mexican wave. "You see, the secret is—"

"Yeah, whatever." A.D. was busy trying on his super-suit. "Hey, not a bad fit."

Suddenly – **BOING!**
– both sides of
Yoki's moustache
stuck up like
quivering clock hands
showing ten to two,
and his eyes
flashed red.

"Whoa." Adventure Duck
backed away. "You're not going to eggs-
plode, are you?"

"**EEEEEEEEEVIL!**" moaned Yoki
in a spooky voice. "The meteor has
affected another animal and made it
EEEEEEEEEVILLLLLL."

- - - - -

Yoki's moustache was working the dial on the satellite radio, and soon a newsreader's voice spoke over the static: "... *eyewitnesses have reported a giant monster striding through the remote farmland, destroying all property in its path ...*"

"I have calculated the co-ordinates," said Yoki, his eyes returning to normal. "I will guide you to the lair of this meteor mutant ... and you must stop him."

"Ah. Mmm. I see." A.D. sighed. "Isn't there anything *easier* I could do?"

"It is never easy to be a hero, young duck."

- - - - -

"What d'you mean, 'young duck'?" A.D. frowned. "You're an egg – I'm older than you are!"

"Only in months and years," Yoki argued.

"All right then, let's get this over with. Hey, maybe that could be my superhero catchphrase? ***LET'S GET THIS OVER WITH!*** Hmm, maybe not. Oh well, it'll come. And I'd better go." A.D. saluted Yoki. "So long, Egg."

And with the echoes of his quack still ringing in the air, he was gone.

Apocalypse, Cow

It was an incredible feeling for a clumsy duck, soaring through the skies like a rocket. Adventure Duck's every feather tingled with energy, and his cape caught the tailwind most impressively. Finally, here was a real adventure!

He looked down at the world below. At first he was only watching out for parks and ponds and soggy bread. But soon he was soaring over wide-open deserts

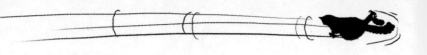

and crowded cities, rivers and rainforests, green fields and purple mountains. Earth was a beautiful place – and A.D. found himself wanting to keep it that way by stopping anyone who threatened it.

Maybe, he thought with some surprise, *I really* could *be a hero!*

"You have reached your destination!" Yoki's voice boomed in A.D.'s mind. "The danger is coming from that large barn below!"

"It is? Oh. Right." A.D. noticed a jagged hole in the barn's roof. "Looks like the meteorite landed right here. I wish I had a catchphrase to help me make a cool entrance." He thought hard. "How about, *TO QUACK-FINITY AND BEYOND!*"

"Er, no," said Yoki.

"Spoilsport!" A.D. complained.

"Dive, dive, dive," Yoki instructed. *"**DIVE!**"*

With the egg's voice ringing in his ears, Adventure Duck spiralled down towards the big barn. He flew in through the hole in the roof and landed in the hayloft. "All right!" he quacked. "*IF YOU WANT A RUCKUS, I'M YOUR DUCKUS!*" He frowned. "Hmm, needs some work."

"And YOU need some manners!" came a deep, gruff voice from down below. "This is MY barn. You should have knocked first."

The owner of the voice rose up on its huge hind legs. It was a cow. A gigantic MEGA-cow, as big as the whole barn!

Adventure Duck found himself standing

face to face with the colossal cow. Her
eyes glowed a luminous green. She
had horns like giant tusks, nostrils like
potholes, hooves like boulders and an
udder as big as a bouncy castle.

A.D. felt his webbed feet go wobbly. "Er, hi!
Seen any glowing rocks lately, Miss ... ?"

"Apocalypse," mooed the beast.
"**APOCALYPSE COW.**"

"Really?" A.D. blinked. "What a, um,
beautiful name."

The cow stared at him blankly, blinking
her strange green eyes.

- - - - -

"Apocalypse means total destruction," Yoki said in his head.

"Right," said A.D. "Well, I'm Adventure Duck." He bunched his feathery fists. "Something tells me you're the evil four-legged force my eggy mate warned me about. So, I'm here to say – whatever you're planning, don't bother! OK?"

"What's that?" wheezed a squeaky voice from the floor of the barn. "Do you

- - - - -

seriously think that the cow is planning something?"

"Who's there?" A.D. demanded. "Are you holding someone prisoner, Cow?" He jumped down from the hayloft ...

... and landed beside a pug with enormous eyes in its flat little face. It was wearing a pinstriped suit and shiny leather shoes. Adventure Duck stared at the tiny, well-dressed dog in amazement.

"You're not seeing things," wheezed the pug. "It's really me."

"Er ... who are you?" asked A.D.

"You *must* know who I am!"

"I don't!"

But then Yoki's voice spoke in his mind. "You have seen this small pug before, young duck ..."

"**WAIT!**" Adventure Duck clapped his wings. "You're that sweet little doggy who sells all the drinks! I've seen you on billboards. And in bins."

- - - - - -

"Bins?" The pug stamped a dinky paw.
"I am **Power Pug**, the official
mascot of POOCHO, INC, the bestselling brand that provides *great-value*
food and drink around the world."

"Power Pug, huh? Wow. You must be worth
a fortune – AHA! Now I get it." A.D. glared
up at Apocalypse Cow. "*That's* why you
kidnapped this cute little fella – for the
ransom! You're making his owners pay to
get him back, aren't you? You evil cow!"

Apocalypse Cow's green eyes flashed in
anger, illuminating the barn.

"You silly duck!" the pug roared. "This

- - - - -

oversized milk-machine is not my jailer ...
she is my underling. My hench-cow!"

The dinky dog's laugh was like a kitten
with a chest infection who'd just stepped
on a mousetrap. "I am the one in charge
here, you foolish waterfowl! **I, Power
Pug – soon to be ruler of
Earth!**"

The Power of the Pug

"Wait a minute," said A.D., confused. "You mean to say this giant cow is working for a little furball like you?"

"I never used to be giant," Apocalypse Cow said slowly. "Until a big rock crashed through the roof of my barn." She moved her hoof to reveal a hole in the ground with a cold, dark chunk of meteor in it.

"Ohhhhhhhhh, I get it," said A.D. "The

meteorite's powers made you super-big –
and the pug really, really titchy."

"HOW DARE YOU!" cried Power Pug,
wheezing in outrage. "I have always been
this size. I am a GIANT
among pugs!"

A.D. nodded. "Riiiiiiiiight."

"And now, thanks to that meteor's amazing
powers, my brainpower has grown to
enormous size too," the pug wheezed,
"along with my hunger for villainy ..."

- - - - -

A.D. suddenly burst out laughing. "Yeah, nice one, pug!" he chuckled. "You almost had me for a second. But you *can't* be the four-legged foe Yoki picked up on. You're way too cute!"

"I am NOT cute!" Power Pug's eyes looked ready to pop. "**I am an evil genius!**"

"Prove it!" A.D. hooted.

"Very well, I will!" Power Pug gave an evil smile. "Have you heard of 'Poocho Moo Juice', the bestselling milk drink in the world?"

"Sure." Adventure Duck nodded. "It has your sweetie-pie face on every bottle."

"Well, since I'm now smarter than Einstein ... and since I've 'persuaded' my owner to put me in charge of Poocho, Inc ... I'm going to make some changes." Power Pug glanced slyly at his giant cow companion. "Starting with the Moo Juice recipe. And once those changes are made, I'll be able to take over the whole wide WORLD.

A·HA·HA·HOOOO·HA·HA·HEEEEEE..."

"OK," said A.D. uneasily, "I'm starting to think you may be serious."

"Well, well – so you're not as stupid as you look." Power Pug stopped laughing and straightened his suit. "Clearly you've been mutated by a meteorite too. Why don't you join Apocalypse Cow and work for me? The whole world will be mine – er, ours!"

"Hmm." Adventure Duck considered the offer. "What's in it for me? Could you start making Moo Juice in Soggy Bread flavour?"

"Certainly not!" Power Pug retorted. "But I *am* planning a new Venison and Biscuit variety."

"Yuk!" Adventure Duck clutched his stomach. "If that's what evil tastes like, I'm definitely using my powers for good."

"Then you will be *beaten* for good," hissed Power Pug. He clapped his paws together. "Apocalypse Cow – *ATTACK!*"

- - - - -

With an earth-rumbling

"**MOOOOOOOO!**" the

giant cow aimed a hoof at Adventure Duck,

who flapped clear just in time.

The blow shattered the wooden wall

behind him.

"Whoa," A.D. called, adjusting his cape.

"I've obviously caught you in a bad

mooooooooooood!"

"I will not tolerate such rubbish puns!"

Power Pug grimaced. "CRUSH HIM, my

hench-animal!"

Apocalypse Cow lashed out with her tail.
WHAP! It coiled around Adventure Duck like
a bionic boa constrictor.

"**OOF!**" Desperately, A.D. tried to pull himself
free but the cow was
much too strong.
"Let's try some
tickle power ..."
He wriggled and
jiggled his soft
feathers against
the meaty coils
of cow tail.

"HURR, HURR, HURR!"
Apocalypse Cow began to rock with loud

laughter, dropping A.D. to the floor. Milk sprayed from her udder like four fire hoses going off.

Adventure Duck beamed. "That's one way to make a milk shake!"

"Gaah! I can't take any more of this duck's dreadful jokes." Power Pug stomped in milky puddles with rage. **"Finish him!"**

"No problem," snarled Apocalypse Cow, her nostrils flaring and her eyes flashing. With a supercharged **SNORT** she blew over a pile of hay bales. They came tumbling down on top of A.D.

- - - - -

"You know what they say ..." Power Pug laughed again. "When it's raining heavy objects – DUCK!"

"Why is everyone better at super-banter than me?" cried Adventure Duck weakly from beneath a heap of hay bales.

"Excellent work, my hench-beast!" panted Power Pug. "That feathery fool will never dare to cross us again! Come, cow! We have much to do. I will milk your powers for all they are worth."

He trotted off, and Apocalypse Cow went lumbering after him, making the whole barn shake.

- - - - -

"**NOOOO**", groaned Adventure Duck beneath the bales of hay. "Those meteor misfits can't get away with this!" He crawled out dizzily and scrambled back to his webbed feet. Adventure Duck could hear the noise of an engine starting up, and ran over to the hole Apocalypse Cow had knocked in the barn wall. To his surprise he saw a sleek plane wheeling across the dusty farmyard.

POOCHO, INC was written on the side of the jet, and a picture of Power Pug stared out from the tailfin. From the bumps and bulges in the metal sides of the plane, it looked as though Apocalypse Cow had somehow squeezed inside.

"Hey!" cried Adventure Duck, running out of the barn. "Come back here!"

But the plane didn't stop. Wobbling wildly with the extra weight, it sped forward, lifted its nose – and shot into the air.

"After them!" boomed Yoki's voice in Adventure Duck's head. "**Don't let the pug get away!**"

Spreading his wings, Adventure Duck leapt into the air and burst into flight.

The chase was on!

Neon Zebra!

Adventure Duck zipped through the air, in hot pursuit of Power Pug's super-jet. He waggled his webbed feet at incredible speed to give himself extra thrust – but Power Pug's plane was rocketing ahead! "Come on," he told himself, "put your feathers into it!"

Flying faster than ever before, A.D. started gaining on the super-jet – until a burst of black smog exploded from the back of it. "Smokescreen!" A.D. choked, his eyes

- - - - -

watering. He spiralled downwards ...

"Young duck!" Yoki's voice rang out in Adventure Duck's mind. "Abort mission! Let the pug and the cow go."

"**WHAT?**" spluttered A.D.

"They are powerful and dangerous," said Yoki. "If we are to fight them, we need allies – and my moustache detects another meteor mutant directly below you."

"*Another* one?" groaned A.D. He swooped out of the black smoke and found himself over a grassy plain under the hot sun. "What am I looking for?"

- - - - -

"I'm not sure," Yoki admitted. "But the meteor has given this animal special powers, **perhaps for good, perhaps for evil**. We must take care."

"What do you mean, 'we'?" A.D. grumbled. "I'm the one taking lumps out here – you're just floating about twiddling your 'tache!"

"Twiddling it in a highly mystical manner," Yoki pointed out, a bit huffily. "And it tells me that you will find the one you seek by the watering hole you're about to splash into."

"Wait – *what?*" As the egg's voice faded

from his head, A.D. suddenly saw the watering hole – coming up fast.

SPLOOSH! Unable to stop in time he made a splashdown, sending waves of water sloshing out in all directions. Sure enough, at the bottom of the pool he saw another enormous rock, its powers drained away.

Poking his head out from beneath the
water like a periscope, he looked around.
On one side of the watering hole he
saw a small herd of dripping-wet zebras
shooting filthy looks his way. And on the

other side, he saw a zebra all on her own.
She wasn't black and white like the rest
of the herd. She was white with luminous
yellow stripes that blazed in the sunlight.

And she was standing on her hind legs.

"OK, Yoki, I'm down," Adventure Duck said. "Now, which one of these zebras am I after?"

"Seriously?" sighed Yoki.

Just then, the zebra with the yellow stripes flashed like she was full of lightning.

Hmm, thought A.D., *maybe it's that one?* He waddled out of the water and approached the strange neon yellow zebra. "Let me guess. Either you've run into a glowing rock recently ... or else you've sat on a mutant egg and you're wishing you'd made an omelette with it."

- - - - - -

"Charming!" said Yoki, at the back of A.D.'s mind.

"You're right about the rock," said the zebra. "It landed here last week when I was taking a drink." She eyed the duck suspiciously. "I'm Ziggy. Who are you?"

"Adventure Duck – but you can call me A.D." He held out a dripping wing for her to shake. "Please to meet– *YAAAAAAAAAGH!*" Sparks flew from the zebra's neon hoof. A.D. snatched back his wing and blew on his scorched feathers. "Ow! What was *that* for?"

"Whoops! My bad," said the zebra. "Are you

- - - - -
76

all right?" Ziggy put a hoof on his back and – **ZAPPP** – A.D. was electrified again! He glowed neon-white, his feathers standing on end.

"OWWWWW! That does it. **QUACK ATTACK!**" Adventure Duck whumped the zebra with his wing.

Ziggy was knocked backwards by the blow.
"No one messes with me, Duckie!"
Furious, she jumped up and flew
at him with a kung-fu kick.
"TASTE MY HOOF!"

Adventure Duck
jumped aside just
in time. "Ha! Your
hoof tastes like
'LOSER'!" he said.
"Let's try your tail
for dessert!" He
grabbed Ziggy by
the tail and spun
her around, faster and
faster. When her legs left

the ground he let go, and the zebra went flying. The other zebras scattered as she landed in a heap in the sticky mud by the side of the watering hole.

"Bad luck, duck!" Ziggy shouted. "Now you've *really* made me mad!" Her stripes blazed shocking pink, burning off all the mud as she pointed her front hooves at him.

"HI-YAAAAAH!"

Neon sparks engulfed Adventure Duck. Gritting his beak against the pain, he tunnelled into the mud to escape. He kept digging until he came out just behind Ziggy – then he grabbed her back legs and wrestled her to the ground.

"**EEEK!**" Struggling, Ziggy rolled over into the watering hole, dragging the duck with her. Electric sparks crackled and the water steamed around them as they grappled. Finally, Ziggy's neon stripes flickered off, fading to a dull blue. Exhausted, Adventure Duck towed the zebra to shore and flopped down in the mud beside her.

"Time out, Duckie?" Ziggy panted.

"Time out," he agreed. "I'm a duck, not a mud wrestler!"

"I didn't mean to hurt you." The zebra sat up and started washing the mud off her stripy fur. "Thing is, I haven't learned to control my new powers yet."

"Yeah, it took me a while too," said A.D., remembering how he'd knocked down the tree by the pond and almost zoomed into outer space. "Sorry I didn't let you explain. I'd just lost a fight against some bad guys – guess I needed to let off some steam."

"Well, we both managed that!" Ziggy pointed to the smoke rising from the water and they laughed. "Bad guys, huh? Does that mean you're a good guy?"

"I'm trying to be." A.D. gave her a crooked smile. "I must be doing something right – I've got an evil arch-enemy and a hench-nemesis, and I've only been in the superhero business a couple of hours!"

"Sounds like fun," Ziggy said wistfully. "More fun than I'm having, anyway. That stupid meteorite messed with my stripes, and now the other zebras avoid me because I keep *zapping* them by accident. What can I do?"

"I know *exactly* what you can do."
Adventure Duck jumped back to his feet.
"You can team up with me and become a
hero!"

"Me?" Ziggy was dumbfounded.

"Why not? **IF I CAN BE A HERO, SO CAN YOU!**"
A.D. beamed at her. "There's a power-mad
pug and a giant cow up to no good ... and
together we can stop them!"

7

Are We Nearly There Yet?

"Listen, thanks for the invite, duck," said Ziggy, "but we only just met. I'm not going anywhere with you. You could be a *total weirdo* for all I know."

"I'm not!" A.D. protested. "Although to be fair, the egg who tries to boss me about is pretty weird."

"Weird?" The air shimmered, and the image of Yoki appeared, floating in front of them. "Weirdness is but an illusion ..."

"Whoa!" Adventure Duck jumped. "Well, I haven't seen him show up like this before, Ziggy, but – meet Yoki. *Everything* is an illusion as far as he's concerned."

"Including illusions," Yoki added wisely. "Greetings, zebra! You are probably wondering how I am able to project an image of myself over incredible distances."

"Actually, I was just wondering who groomed your moustache," Ziggy admitted.

- - - - -

"It's even longer and bushier than my mane."

"And, I think you'll find, shinier too!" Yoki cleared his throat. "Er, anyway ... It is in fact my super-powerful brainwaves that allow me to beam my image, live, to you now. Adventure Duck needs your help to fight Power Pug and his hench-animal, Apocalypse Cow."

Holographic images of both baddies hovered in the air in front of Ziggy. She jumped, and a crackle of green energy zapped out of her behind. "**WHOOPS!**"

"Better out than in," A.D. told her. "These

- - - - -

are the charmers I was telling you about.
I was chasing their jet when I dropped in
on you."

"Which way were they going?" asked
Ziggy.

Adventure Duck thought hard. "Er,
through the sky."

Ziggy glared at him. "Very helpful!"

"Let us go over what we *do* know," said
Yoki, "for only truth may show us ... er,
the truth." He closed his eyes and the
images of Power Pug and Apocalypse Cow
vanished. "Well, young duck?"

"Power Pug said he was going to change the Moo Juice recipe and take over the world," A.D. recalled.

"Well, if that plug-ugly pug wants to change the recipe, he'll have to get to the dairy where they make the stuff," Ziggy reasoned. "So why don't we just go there and stop them?"

Yoki and Adventure Duck looked at each other, impressed.

"I wish I'd thought of that!" said A.D.

"She is wise," said Yoki. "Especially for a zebra."

"Don't patronise me, you omelette-in-training!" Ziggy growled. "Find the factory. Get cracking!"

"It shall be done." Yoki closed his eyes in concentration.

"So, Zig, I guess you're joining us, yeah?" Adventure Duck beamed. "Check me – I've got a sidekick!"

"**SIDEKICK?**" Ziggy booted him with her back hoof. "Call me 'sidekick' again, you'll GET a side-kick!"

"OK, OK!" said A.D., rubbing his ribs.
"I meant '*crime-fighting partner*', obvs."

- - - - -

"That's better. And as your crime-fighting partner, I need a costume too." Ziggy ripped a strip of fabric from the end of A.D.'s cape and tied it around her forehead. "That'll do! One brilliant bandana – for me, the even more brilliant **NEON ZEBRA!**"

Adventure Duck nodded approvingly. "Cool superhero name."

Yoki's only comment was a straining sound. He started to shake.

"Whoa there," said A.D. "Everything OK?"

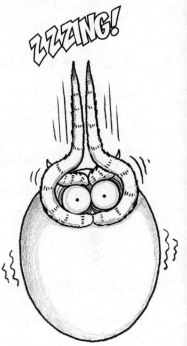

"GOT IT!" Yoki's moustache twanged straight up in the air. "I have located the Poocho Dairy, where Moo Juice is produced."

A.D. gulped. "Then ... we'd better get straight there."

"Yep!" Ziggy straightened her bandana and fired up her stripes. "It's time for Adventure Duck and Neon Zebra to fight evil together – er, as long as you can give me a lift."

- - - - -

A.D. frowned. "I just hope you're lighter than you look."

"Of course I'm light." Ziggy zapped him in the face with a bright pink spark. "NEON light!"

"Ouch! Very funny," grumbled Adventure Duck. "Come on, then, climb aboard. When it comes to saving the world, there's no ducking out."

"Or zebra-ing out," Ziggy added. "LET'S GO!"

"Are we nearly there yet?" asked Ziggy for

what seemed like the thousandth time.

"**NO!**" snapped A.D. "Just like I told you two minutes ago." Flying for hundreds of miles with an electric zebra on your back was tiring. When that zebra was also singing terrible made-up songs to pass the time, it was completely exhausting!

A.D. tried to keep calm and carry on as they raced to the Poocho Dairy. Things were going quite well too, until, somewhere over the ocean, Ziggy invented a particularly annoying power-ballad called 'Zoom':

"Zoom, Duckie, zoom!
So we can do a BOOM!
BOOM! ZAP! ZAP!
Then everyone will clap!
And we can take a nap!
So zoom, Duckie, zoom!
And we can do a BOOOOOOM!"

"That's terrible!" groaned Adventure Duck. "What even is a BOOM?"

"**BOOM***!*" Ziggy thumped him round the head. "*That* is."

All in all, it was quite a long journey.

They arrived in a busy city just as night was falling – and A.D. almost fell too, down to the ground with exhaustion.

"Turn left!" Yoki's voice was back in Adventure Duck's head. "The factory we seek is just a few blocks from here ..."

"Who needs sat nav when you've got an egg with a hairy top lip?" A.D. said. "Battling Power Pug and Apocalypse Cow will seem like a holiday after this trip!"

But as A.D. soared over the skyscrapers, he knew that was not true. The last time he'd tangled with those evil meteor mutants, it was nearly game over. *I must be crazy to face them again*, he thought, *even with an easily provoked electric zebra on my side.*

"Do not be afraid, young duck," Yoki murmured in his mind. "If you fail, it's not the end of the world. Power Pug will merely take over the planet and make every living creature his slave."

Before A.D. could thank him with a heavy dose of sarcasm, Ziggy piped up: "Hey, look!" She pointed to a large, square building crowned with giant flashing milk bottles.

"There it is, the Poocho Dairy!"

Hundreds of delivery trucks were parked outside the building. "They must be getting ready to ship out the new-recipe Moo Juice," said Adventure Duck. He gasped as he noticed another vehicle parked by the trucks. "And there's Power Pug's private jet!"

"Then the bad guys are already here," said Ziggy nervously.

"That's right." Adventure Duck nodded. **"LET'S GO AND BE HEROES!"**

Udder Disaster

A.D. and Ziggy landed on the dairy roof beside a skylight. Inside, bright lights shone down on a long conveyor belt lined with bottles. The bottles were being filled from a vast vat of milk. There was no sign of anyone about.

"We'd better get in there," said Adventure Duck. "I have to admit, I've got butterflies in my stomach."

"Why the heck did you eat butterflies? You weirdo!" Ziggy charged up her stripes until they glowed electric orange.

"Cool colour," said A.D. "Not seen that shade before."

"Nor have I. But I reckon it means I'm ... READY FOR ACTION!" She jumped in the air and smashed through the skylight, shouting "**NEON ZEB-RAAAAAH**-RAH-RAH-RAH!"

"Seriously?" A.D. yelled. "We could've sneaked in through a window or something!"

- - - - -

As he flapped down after her, A.D. realised the room was actually twice as big as the part you could see through the skylight. And in the part you *couldn't*, there stood Apocalypse Cow, staring into space with her glowing green eyes. Her oversized udder was hooked up to a juddering milking machine. Creamy milk gushed into a gigantic glass vat, supervised by four humans in long white coats.

Ziggy landed next to the vat. "All right, you lot," she shouted. "Turn off the machine, or taste Neon Zebra's **hooves of hurt!**"

"And taste my webbed feet of, er, 'not

very nice'," Adventure Duck added, landing beside Ziggy. "Sorry, that wasn't very good. Shall I come in again?"

"I wouldn't bother," said Ziggy, looking around. "No one's even noticed us!"

A.D. saw that she was right. The humans at the controls hadn't even looked up, and Apocalypse Cow was still staring into space. "This is a bit odd," he said. "I wonder where that ratty little dog has gone?"

"We have to sort him out, super-fast," said Ziggy. "There's no time to lose."

"Wrong!" A wheezing chuckle made them

turn around. "There's definitely time for YOU to lose."

Power Pug stood behind them. He was no longer dressed in his business suit. Now he wore a top hat, a black suit with a sparkly waistcoat and a red-lined cloak.

"SICK OUTFIT, BRO,"

said A.D, straight-faced.

"When taking over the world," said Power Pug, preening, "it's important to dress correctly."

"So what went wrong? You look like a vampire who joined a circus."

The pug narrowed his eyes, his little pink tongue lolling from the side of his mouth. "You were most unwise to face me a second time, duck," he hissed. "You think this garish zebra can protect you from my wrath?"

"I just hope she can wake me up when your threats bore me to sleep." A.D. smiled. "She got powers from the meteor, same as we did – and I've made her my side ... er, partner!"

"You'd better believe it, pug!" snarled Ziggy. "Whatever you're up to, we're going to stop it!"

- - - - - -

A.D. nodded. "Actually, it would be helpful if you could explain exactly what it is you are up to. With diagrams."

SCRATCH

"HA!" Power Pug puffed himself up to his full, unimpressive height. "And if I refuse?"

"We'll trash this whole dairy." Ziggy's stripes glowed extra bright as she raised a hoof and jabbed it against the conveyor belt. Electric sparks shot through the equipment and – **KA-BOOOOOM!** –

the conveyor belt rattled to a halt, smoke pouring out of the machinery. "See?"

A.D. braced himself for aggro from Apocalypse Cow, but the giant creature didn't move a muscle. She just stared into space with those eerily vacant green eyes.

"Your talents are impressive, zebra ... but ultimately useless." Power Pug wagged his tail to waft away the smoke. "Repair the conveyor belt!" he ordered the humans.

"**Yes, master!**" chorused the workers.

"What's wrong with these people?" cried A.D. "A glowing zebra and a duck in daring pants start wrecking their factory and they don't even bat an eyelid."

"Indeed they do not." The diminutive dog smiled, revealing a single bright white fang. "Tell me ... why do you think I am called Power Pug?"

"Because your mum couldn't spell 'Bum Face'?" Ziggy suggested.

"I will *show* you why." The pug's eyes started to swirl with eerie light. "You see, as well as super-brainpower and super-villainy ... the meteorite has given me the power of ... *mind control!*"

"What?" Adventure Duck was growing dizzy. He frowned and forced himself to look away. "**ZIGGY, WATCH OUT. HE'S TRYING TO HYPNOTISE YOU!**"

But it was too late. Ziggy was in some sort of trance. Her eyes turned a luminous, glowing green.

"Just like Apocalypse Cow," A.D. gasped, suddenly realising. "She's been under Power Pug's mind control the whole time!"

"You work for me now, Neon Zebra," wheezed Power Pug. "Your electric energy will provide power for Poocho, Inc ..."

"**Yes, master,**" said Ziggy slowly.

"Stop that!" Adventure Duck staggered forward and whumped Power Pug with a wing. The dog rolled over backwards, and A.D. grabbed Ziggy by the shoulders, staring into her shining eyes. "Neon Zebra, can you hear me? Wake up!"

"You're too late, duck!" sneered Power Pug. "Now I have TWO hench-animals who will obey me without question."

Adventure Duck looked at the giant cow and back again. "I always wondered why she let a shrimp like you boss her around."

"She has no choice!" said Power Pug, rubbing his paws and chortling with glee. "She is completely under my mind control ... which means the milk she makes is **Mind Control Milk!**"

- - - - -

"And now you're using it to make Moo Juice!" A.D. groaned. "Millions of people drink that stuff all over the world."

"And once they've drunk it, they will fall under my control." Power Pug's voice was growing higher. "I will broadcast a message on television, urging them to overthrow their rulers ... The world will fall into *CHAOS* ... and only Power Pug will be able to pick up the pieces."

"I don't think so!" A.D. adjusted his pants and cape. "Because *I'm* going to stop you."

"Ha!" Power Pug clapped his paws. "Cow! Zebra! Attack this feathered fool!"

- - - - -

Adventure Duck gulped. "Uh-oh!"

Apocalypse Cow jerked awake and
lumbered to her feet, the milking machine
falling from her udder, her face a picture
of pure rage.

Neon Zebra turned slowly to A.D. and raised her hooves, her stripes glowing bright red.

"Destroy the duck, my puppets," cried Power Pug. "**AT ONCE!**"

Dairy of Doom

ZAPPPPP! Neon Zebra unleashed a jolt of electricity at Adventure Duck. He flapped out of the way and the ruby-red sparks scorched a hole in the wall behind him. But in making his escape, he flew too close to Apocalypse Cow.

POW! Her hoof swatted A.D. like a fly, and he crashed to the floor.

"Hi-YAAAAAAH!" Neon Zebra

launched herself into a flying jump kick.
A.D. barely rolled clear in time – and
as a shadow fell over him, he realised
Apocalypse Cow's hoof was dropping down
to stomp him into a duck pancake.

Desperately, A.D.
dived aside –
into another of
Neon Zebra's
zaps. This one
caught him
square on the
chest and blew
him backwards
into the vat
of milk.

SLAMMMM! He slid down it slowly, his head spinning.

"You can't hope to survive, duck!" snarled Power Pug. "Why not beg me on your knees for forgiveness? I may show mercy!"

"OK ..." Adventure Duck crouched down and put both wings together. "I beg you, Power Pug. Please ... *SHUT YOUR FACE!*" He launched into the air like a rocket and socked Apocalypse Cow under the chin. **POW!** Caught off-guard, the cow staggered backwards. "Next time, pick on someone your own size!" taunted Adventure Duck. "Like, er, the planet Jupiter ..."

- - - - -

POW-**POW**-**POW**! Adventure

Duck followed up his sneak attack with some wing-whacks to the cow's belly and a beak-bash to her behind. Finally, he took

a deep breath and let rip with a really
enormous, earth-quaking

QUACK!

The noise reverberated around the factory.

Windows exploded.

Cracks riddled the walls.

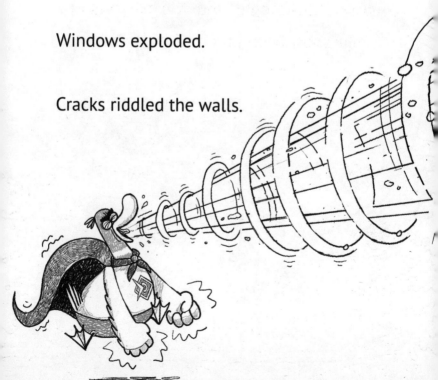

The human workers were thrown to the floor.

Power Pug whined and hid under the conveyor belt.

Apocalypse Cow's green eyes began to flicker. Reeling and clutching her ears, the massive cow toppled into the giant vat of milk she'd been filling with a terrific

"Get out of that, you stupid cow!" Power Pug yelled, peeping out from his cover. **"You'll ruin the flavour!"**

A.D. flapped to the factory floor, panting for breath. But –

– Ziggy shot a blast of crackling neon energy straight at him.

"WHOAAAA!" Adventure Duck somersaulted through the air and landed on the conveyor belt, knocking Moo Juice bottles everywhere. "Come on, Zig, snap out of it! We're meant to be partners, remember?"

But Ziggy was still under Power Pug's control. The hypnotised zebra jumped on to the conveyor belt beside A.D. and raised her hooves, ready to deliver a final, frazzling super-zap ...

Adventure Duck knew it was time to take drastic action.

"Wait! What am I saying?" he said with a smile. "We're *not* partners. You're my ...

SIDEKICK!"

Ziggy froze and blinked. "Wh ... what?"

"My stripy sidekick," A.D. cried. "That's you, that is!"

"Wait." Ziggy shook her head, scowling, the green glow fading from her eyes. "WHAT did you say ... ?"

"Are your ears blocked?" Power Pug cried, crawling out from under the conveyor belt. "He said that you are his *SIDEKICK*, you silly zebra—"

"*NO ONE CALLS ME A SIDEKICK!*" bellowed Ziggy. With her eyes alert and black again, Ziggy pounced on Power Pug.

- - - - -

He squealed as she picked him up and hurled him into the air. "**WHEEEEE!**"

Just then, Apocalypse Cow lifted her enormous head out of the vat – and the little pug shot up her left nostril. His little back paws kicked about helplessly, like a bogey trying to break free.

"Phew! Welcome back, partner!" Adventure Duck beamed at Ziggy. "I hoped that if I made you mad enough, it would break through the pug's hypnotic control."

"Well, you picked the right way to do it, *partner*." She winked at him, and then stared sternly up at Apocalypse Cow. "Now, let's finish this!"

"No." The cow rose up from inside the vat like a tower, milk dripping off her. "Let **ME** finish this."

Exhausted but determined to go down fighting, Adventure Duck braced himself for another battle.

Apocalypse Cow raised her humungous hoof ...

... and put it to her nose.

HOOONNNK! Apocalypse Cow blew hard and Power Pug popped out of her nostril like a cork from a bottle.

CRASH! He hit the ground, leaving a small crater.

"What do you think you're doing?" Power Pug squeaked, eyes boggling. "You are my hench-cow. You are under my control."

"I *was* under your control," Apocalypse Cow

agreed, nodding her enormous head. "But then—"

"My supersonic quack jolted you awake!" A.D. cheered.

"Actually, no," said the cow. "I swallowed some of the mind-control milk. Since my mind was already being controlled, I guess the two things cancelled each other out."

"Oh," said Adventure Duck, disappointed.

"But I never would've fallen in here if not for you, so thanks." Apocalypse Cow smiled at Adventure Duck, then glowered at Power Pug. "To think a peaceful young

- - - - -

cow like me almost helped a naughty little doggy like you take control of the world!"

"I *am* thinking about it," said Power Pug, a dreamy smile on his face.

"Well, now your plans have been canned and your creamy dreams are over." Ziggy raised a hoof. "**HIIII-YAAAAAH!**" She kung-fu kicked the milk vat, and cracks spread through the glass.

"I like your style," said Apocalypse Cow, and kicked the glass from the inside.

CRACK! The vat broke apart with a crash.

- - - - -

WHOOSH! A tidal wave of milk flooded out into the dairy!

"**YIKES!**" quacked A.D., flapping into the air to avoid it.

But Power Pug was not so lucky. "**Nooooooooooooo!**" he wailed as the mass of milk washed him out of the dairy. "You haven't heard the last of me," he yelled as he was sluiced towards the sewers. "I shall returrrrrrnnnnnnnnnn!"

"Good!" Adventure Duck shouted after him. "We can always use a laugh!"

"Look at him go," giggled Apocalypse Cow. "Like a bug down a plughole."

"Or a pug down a *pug*hole!" Ziggy suggested.

And then, in a swirl of mind-control milk, Power Pug disappeared down the drain!

Heroes' Return

Adventure Duck looked around the milk-splattered dairy. There were feathers, pieces of shattered glass and puddles of milk everywhere. The human workers coughed and started to revive.

"They will recover now, just like I did," said the cow. "I'm sorry I fought you. My name isn't even Apocalypse Cow – it's Edna."

"Don't worry, Edna. We know that Power

Pug was controlling you," A.D. said with a smile. "Are you going back to your barn now?"

"Actually, I'm going to take Power Pug's private plane and travel the world protecting farm animals in need," Edna declared.

"What about you?" A.D. asked Ziggy. "Do you want to go back to the watering hole?"

"Are you kidding?" said Ziggy, her stripes glowing pink. "We're partners. Wherever you go, I go."

A.D. frowned. "Even to the toilet?"

- - - - -

"Er, no," said Ziggy quickly. "But, you know, fighting crime and stuff ..."

"I do know," said A.D., smiling, "and it's cool with me. You can come back to the pond and stay with me and Yoki."

"I will give you a lift," Edna declared. "But let's go now, shall we?" She nodded at the humans, who were still waking up. "Before we have to answer a lot of awkward questions."

"Good plan," said Adventure Duck. "The mind-control milk's gone down the drain, the world is saved – I reckon our work here is done!"

Back at the pond in the park, in the quiet of dawn, Yoki was waiting with great excitement for A.D. to return.

Presently, a bulging plane flew overhead. The pug logo on the tailfin had been replaced with a picture of a smiling cow. "**DUCKABUNGA!**" came a cry from on high, as a feathered figure jumped from a window.

"Neon Zeb-RAH-RAH-RAH!" yelled Ziggy as she leapt from the plane's rear doorway with a parachute on her back.

- - - - -

Yoki waved his moustache at them.

"Welcome, heroic animals!"

"We were pretty heroic, weren't we?"
Adventure Duck said, beaming his beak off.
"Especially me!"

"And me!" **THUMP!** Ziggy landed

on the grass and her deflating parachute completely covered A.D. She started cropping the long grass. "Hey, nice place you've got here. First I amaze, then I can graze!"

"You have both done very well." Yoki smiled serenely at A.D. as the duck crawled out from under the parachute. "I am sure your careers will be long and highly heroic."

"Apocalypse Cow – I mean, Edna – was a hero as well," said A.D., watching as the jet disappeared from sight. "Turns out she's a great pilot, too. We only nearly crashed into buildings four times on the way home!" He put a wing around Yoki. "So how are you doing, egg-head? Did you have a nice rest while Zig and I saved the world?"

"REST?" Yoki's moustache shot up into the air. "On the contrary ... I have been busy upgrading the **Underpond.**"

Ziggy frowned. "The Under-what?"

"At least you didn't ask about the Underwear!" said A.D. with a grin. "**WHOA!**"

Yoki pulled on the bulrush lever and the ground tipped upside down, plunging all three heroes into a much larger

- - - - -

underground burrow. Interesting levers and switches stuck out from both feathery floor and slimy ceiling, and strange gadgets littered the space.

"Hey, this is a cool base!" Ziggy said. "In fact, it's downright chilly. I'm from Africa – can't you put a heater on or something?"

"Of course." Yoki nudged a switch and a bright, warming bulb lit up in the roof. Ziggy sighed happily as she basked in its warm glow.

"You got a brand new TV in here!" A.D.'s eyes were wide as saucers as he gazed around. "And two games consoles, and

a gym, and ... is that a **SOGGY BREAD DISPENSER** over there?"

"It may be," Yoki said with a smile. "If you are to risk your life in the battle against mutant animals again, you deserve to enjoy yourself while off duty."

"Well, my off-duty booty thanks you." A.D. sank down on to the soft, feathery floor. "Wait – I have to risk my life *again?*"

"I guess we both do, partner," Ziggy murmured.

"I sense that Power Pug will be back," Yoki explained. "And there are many more mutant animals out there, affected by the meteor ... I fear that not all of them will be as nice as the two of you."

"You old charmer!" Ziggy whumped Yoki fondly with a hoof, nearly cracking his shell. "Well, you know what I say? **BRING IT, BAD GUYS!**"

"Yeah, bring it," Adventure Duck agreed. "And then take it away again – or you'll be sorry!" As he switched on the huge TV, he felt truly happy. All in all, it had been a pretty good couple of days. He'd made some cool friends ... and faced some wild enemies. Best of all, he had gained some incredible powers and he'd used them to save the world.

- - - - -

Even if his catchphrases could use some work, Adventure Duck knew that he was a fully fledged superhero! And whenever danger called, he would come waddling to save the day.

THE END

STEVE COLE

Bestselling author Steve Cole comes from a village with three different duck ponds. None of them has been hit by a meteor, but a duck did attack him once! When he's not writing funny stories, Steve plays bass in a pop band. Steve has a pet dog named Clara, who luckily does not possess evil mind-control powers. The superpower Steve would most like is the ability to conjure chocolate and chips from thin air (not always at the same time).

ALEKSEI BITSKOFF

Illustrator Aleksei Bitskoff was born in Estonia and loved to draw as a child, covering his school exercise books in doodles. He planned to become a teacher, but his travels brought him to London where he studied illustration instead. The superpower he would like most is self-multiplication, so he could be in lots of different places at the same time!

Ready...
steady...
soggy bready!

Look out for ADVENTURE DUCK'S
next action-packed mission in...

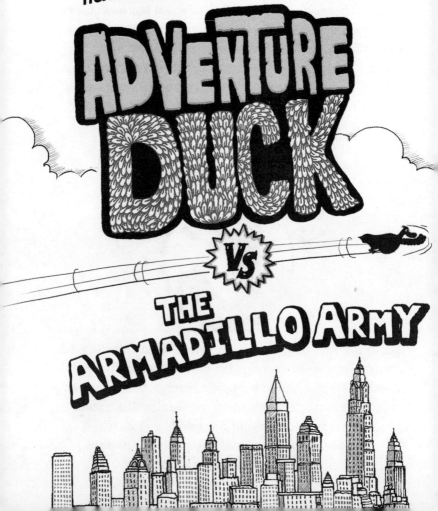

ADVENTURE
DUCK
VS
THE
ARMADILLO ARMY